Editor Frankie Hallam
Project Art Editor Jon Hall
Production Editor Marc Staples
Senior Production Controller Laura Andrews
Managing Editor Emma Grange
Managing Art Editor Vicky Short
Managing Director Mark Searle

Designed for DK by Thelma-Jane Robb
Reading Consultant Barbara Marinak

First American Edition, 2025
Published in the United States by DK Publishing,
1745 Broadway, 20th Floor, New York, NY 10019

© 2025 MARVEL

Page design copyright © 2025 Dorling Kindersley Limited
DK, a Division of Penguin Random House LLC
25 26 27 28 29 10 9 8 7 6 5 4 3 2 1
001–345009–Feb/2025

All rights reserved.
Without limiting the rights under the copyright reserved above, no part of this publication may be reproduced, stored in or introduced into a retrieval system, or transmitted, in any form, or by any means (electronic, mechanical, photocopying, recording, or otherwise), without the prior written permission of the copyright owner.
Published in Great Britain by Dorling Kindersley Limited

A catalog record for this book
is available from the Library of Congress.
ISBN 978-0-5939-6079-0 (Paperback)
ISBN 978-0-5939-6080-6 (Hardcover)

DK books are available at special discounts when purchased
in bulk for sales promotions, premiums, fund-raising, or educational use.
For details, contact: DK Publishing Special Markets,
1745 Broadway, 20th Floor, New York, NY 10019
SpecialSales@dk.com

Printed and bound in China

www.dk.com

This book was made with Forest Stewardship Council™ certified paper—one small step in DK's commitment to a sustainable future. Learn more at www.dk.com/uk/information/sustainability

Go Team Spidey!

Frankie Hallam

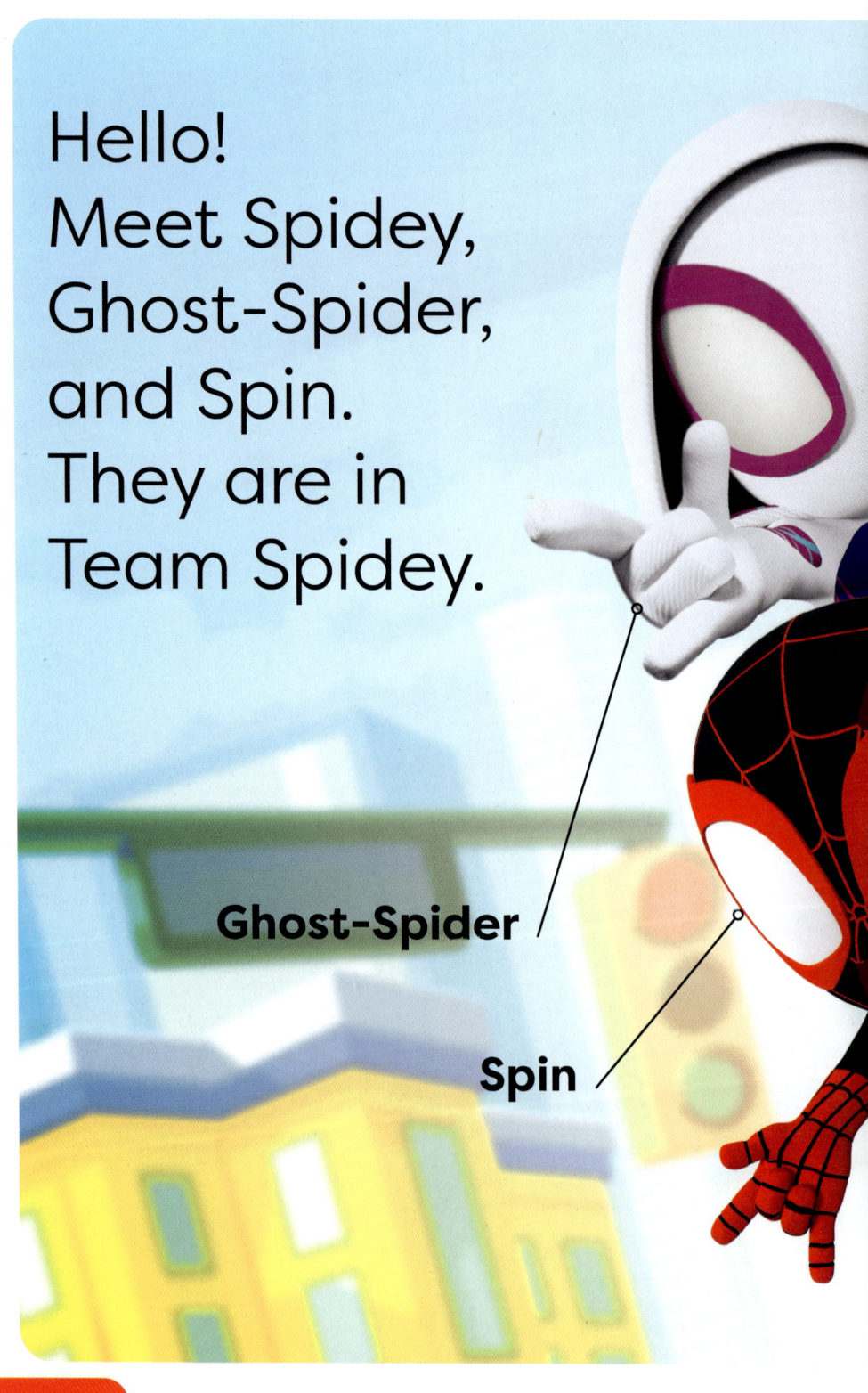

Hello!
Meet Spidey,
Ghost-Spider,
and Spin.
They are in
Team Spidey.

Ghost-Spider

Spin

This is Spidey. Spidey's real name is Peter.

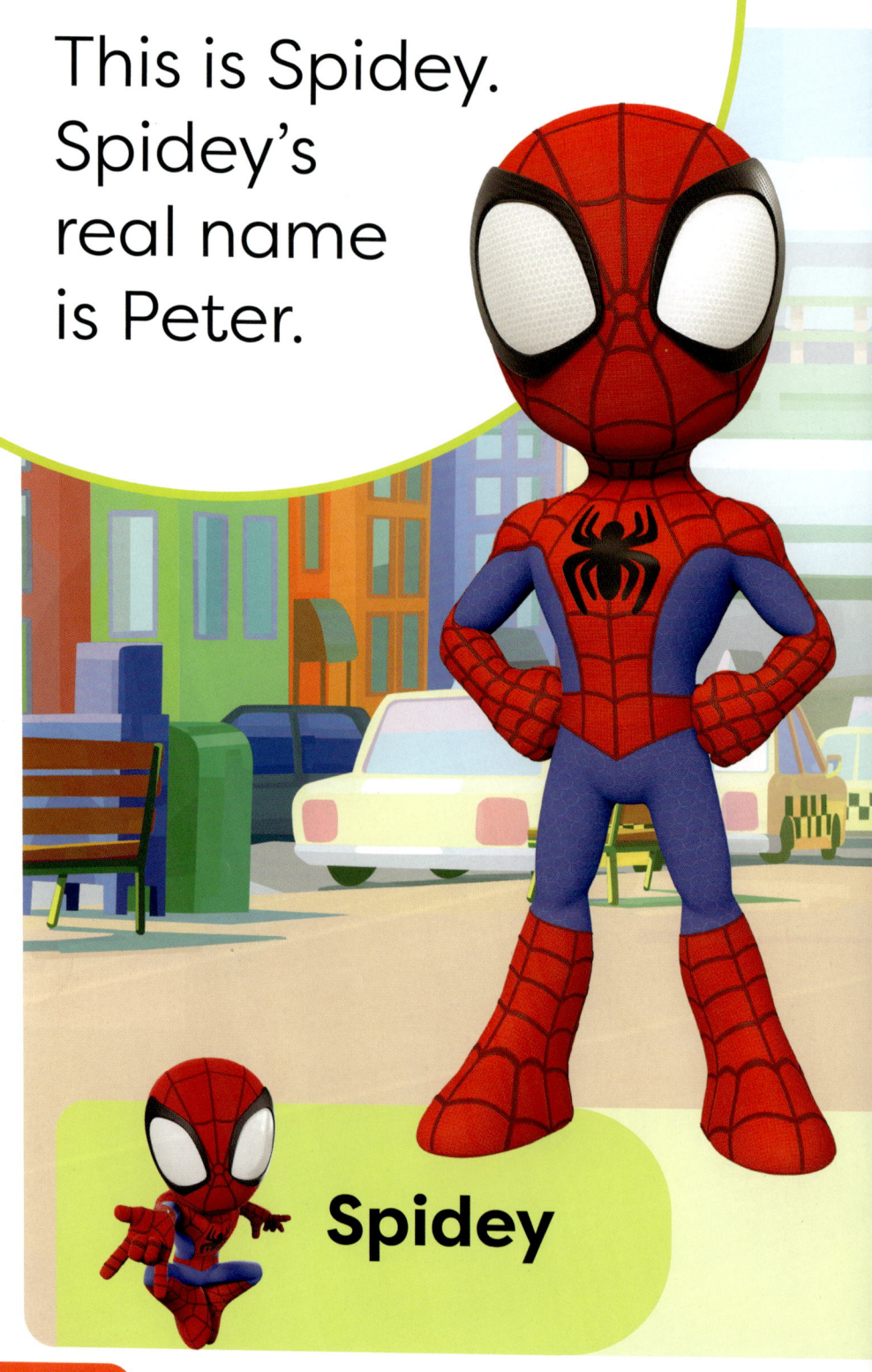

Spidey

Peter is good at science. He is smart.

Spin

This is Spin.
Spin is Spidey's friend.
His real name is Miles.
Spin is a hero.

This is Ghost-Spider.
Her real name is Gwen.
Gwen is brave.

Ghost-Spider

Team Spidey uses webs. The webs can glow.

Go Team Spidey!

webs

Watch them swing.
Swish!

Team Spidey has many friends. Here they are. They take a selfie.

Black Panther

Reptil

This is Ms. Marvel.
Her body stretches.

Look! Her arm is getting longer.

Ms. Marvel

Iron Man is strong.
He wears a suit.
It is red and gold.
He flies. Zoom!

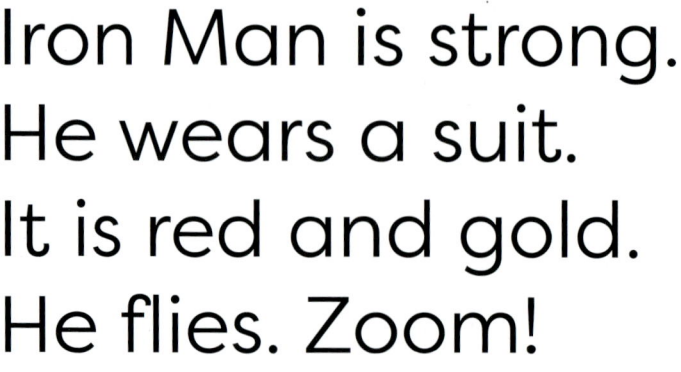

Iron Man

Here comes trouble! These villains are bad. Team Spidey must stop them.

Doc Ock

Green Goblin

villains

This is Green Goblin.
He is cheeky.
He plays tricks
on Team Spidey.

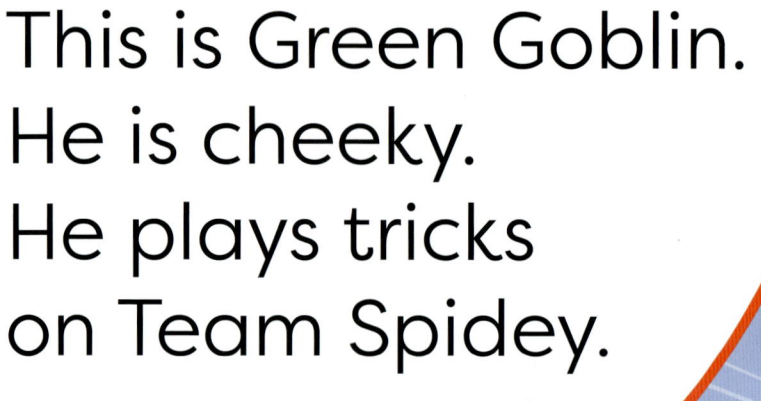

Green Goblin

Watch out!
Rhino is near.
Stomp! Crash! Thump!
Team Spidey will
save the day.

Rhino

What's that noise?
Vroom!
It's Team Spidey.

Spidey drives his car.

copter

Ghost-Spider flies her copter.

Spin rides his bike.

This team works together. It never gives up.

Go Team Spidey!

team

Goodbye, Team Spidey!
See you soon.

Glossary

Webs
Threads that are spun by spiders

Friends
People who you like and know well

Villains
Bad people who act in a mean way

Copter
A machine that people can use to fly

Team
A group formed to work together

Quiz

Answer the questions to see what you have learned. Check your answers with an adult.

1. Who are the members of Team Spidey?
2. What is Spin's real name?
3. How many colors are on Iron Man's suit?
4. What is Ms. Marvel's power?
5. If you could be a Super Hero, what would your power be?

1. Spidey, Spin, and Ghost-Spider 2. Miles 3. Two (red and gold)
4. Her body can stretch 5. Answers will vary